D1627041

THE PRINCESS AND THE FOX

A.M. Luzzader

Illustrated by Anna M. Clark

Published by Knowledge Forest Press

P.O. Box 6331

Logan, UT 84341

Ebook ISBN-13: 978-1-949078-77-0

Paperback ISBN-13: 978-1-949078-76-3

Cover design by Sleepy Fox Studio, www.sleepyfoxstudio.net

Editing by Chadd VanZanten

Interior illustrations by Anna M. Clark, annamclarkart.com

To Olivia, beautiful and brilliant lover of foxes.
—A.M.L.

To my brother-in-law, Braydn, for his support and genuine interest in my artistic projects. —A.M.C.

The real-life Princess Olivia and Princess Juniper

CONTENTS

CHAPTER ONE

SYLVIA THE FOX

In a faraway place, in a faraway time, there was once a place called Wildflower Kingdom. It was named that because of the many wildflowers that grew there in red, yellow, blue, and purple.

But the flowers in Wildflower Kingdom weren't the only beautiful things there. Many things about the Kingdom were beautiful. For example, in the village of Wildflower Kingdom, there were many pretty houses and shops. The houses had colorful shutters and window boxes filled with flowers. The shops had fancy signs and charming window displays. There were cobblestone roads running from place to place.

There was also Wildflower Castle, which was very tall, with colorful banners and a beautiful courtyard.

On the western side of the kingdom, there was a beach where the setting sun turned the sky magenta, purple, and pink.

But there was one part of Wildflower Kingdom that was not only beautiful, but it was an amazing place for all of the senses. This place was Wildflower Forest. It stood on the edge of Wildflower Kingdom, near Stony Mountain, where Patrick the Dragon lived.

If you were to stroll through Wildflower Forest, you would notice how the ground felt soft in some places because of fallen pine needles. You would smell pine and cedar and rich forest soil. You would hear the wind moving through the trees. You would hear birds singing and squirrels chattering in the treetops.

The forest was also home to deer, rabbits, and bears, though you might not see them.

In the summer, when it was hot outside, the forest was a great place to cool off. The forest was shaded from the sun and there were many cool, grassy groves.

A sparkling brook flowed through Wildflower Forest. The brook flowed over colorful rocks, making a relaxing water noise. Wildflower Forest had a walking path, too, and a bridge that crossed the brook.

Many people enjoyed walking through the forest, and that included the two princesses of Wildflower Kingdom, Princess Olivia and Princess Juniper.

Princess Olivia and Princess Juniper were part of the royal family of Wildflower Castle. Their mother was Queen Jennifer. She had long hair and loved to read books and do arts and crafts. Olivia and Juniper's father was King Andrew. He had a dark beard and enjoyed painting toy soldiers in his spare time.

Princess Olivia was the older of the two sisters. She was eight years old, and she liked to be in charge. She had a wonderful imagination. It was easy for her to imagine fairies or mermaids or other fantastical creatures. She liked to pretend that she was their friend and caretaker.

Princess Juniper was the younger sister. She was six years old, and she also liked to be in charge. Juniper liked to run fast. Very fast. Sometimes she pretended that she was one of the many unicorns that roamed the kingdom.

Queen Jennifer

King Andrew

Princess Olivia

Princess Juniper

Juniper even tried grazing on the lush green grasses that grew in the wildflower meadows. She didn't like this very much. She had to spit it out, and she decided that she preferred the food prepared by Miss Beets, the castle chef. Juniper even decided that she would eat all her vegetables before she'd eat grass again.

One day, right after the princesses had finished their morning chores and eating breakfast, their father came to speak with them.

"I was thinking," said King Andrew. "That today might be a nice day to visit Wildflower Forest. We could walk along the trail and look for the new wildflowers, what do you think about that?"

"Oh, yes, please," said Olivia. "I love going to the forest to hear the birds singing!"

"Yes, let's go!" said Juniper. "I love to smell the trees and put my feet in the brook."

"Very well," said King Andrew. "Perhaps we should invite some friends as well. Perhaps Paul and Sylvia?"

Olivia's eyes grew wide. "That will be amazing!"

"It will be fantastic!" said Juniper.

Paul was a candlestick maker who lived and worked in the village of Wildflower Kingdom.

Paul made tall, skinny candles that could burn for a very long time. He also made short, colorful candles in small glass jars that made wonderful odors, like vanilla and blueberry. Olivia's favorite candle scent was strawberry. Juniper's favorite was lilac.

Paul was tall and had orange hair and an orange beard. His eyes always twinkled, and he always seemed happy. Paul was a very kind man and a good friend of King Andrew and the rest of the royal family.

Sylvia wasn't a person at all. She was a fox! Sylvia lived with Paul. He fed her and took care of Sylvia. It's unusual for a fox to live with a human. However, Paul had found Sylvia after she'd been injured. Sylvia was very young at the time and needed help. Paul brought her to his home to help Sylvia recover from her injury. She had stayed with Paul ever since.

Sylvia had bright eyes, a small nose, and large ears. The orange fur on her back and tail was almost the same color as Paul's hair and beard. She also had white fur on her face and belly. The fur on the tips of her ears was black, and so was the tip of her long, fluffy tail.

Sylvia had an excellent sense of smell. One time, when Sparkles the unicorn had been sick, Sylvia had used her nose to help find a marshmallow plant to make medicine for Sparkles.

When King Andrew invited Paul and Sylvia to join them on their visit to the forest, there was much excitement. Olivia and Juniper were excited because they loved playing with Sylvia. It would make the visit to the forest even more fun. No one could say exactly how Sylvia felt, because she couldn't speak. But she really seemed excited. Sylvia jumped up and down and wagged her tail.

Paul and Sylvia met the princesses and their father at the beginning of the forest trail.

"How are the princesses?" Paul asked.

"Very well, thank you," said Princess Olivia.

"Yeah, especially now that we get to see Sylvia," said Juniper. "We love Sylvia!"

Juniper and Olivia patted the fox on her head.

While King Andrew and Paul walked down the forest path, they chatted about the things they had been doing recently.

Paul told King Andrew about some new candle scents he was developing. King Andrew told Paul about the business of the kingdom. They walked very slowly so they could keep talking.

The princesses found all this grown-up talk and slow-walking very boring. They wanted to run!

"You may run ahead," King Andrew told them. "But don't go too far."

The princesses ran ahead. Then they ran back to their father and Paul. Then they ran ahead again. Back and forth they ran. Sylvia ran with them.

Foxes don't smile exactly, at least not in the way humans do, but they knew that Sylvia was having fun. She ran and hopped and yipped happily.

The princesses both loved Wildflower Castle and the nearby village, but something about the forest made them feel more alive. Perhaps it was the cool, fresh air. Or maybe it was the splashing sound of the brook. Or was it the birdsong? Maybe it was all of these things together.

Everyone was smiling and laughing. It started out as a happy day, but no one knew that something would soon happen to make it a very sad day.

CHAPTER TWO

LOST IN THE FOREST

When Olivia and Juniper reached the bridge over the babbling brook, they stopped for a while. They had a fun game that they often played at the bridge. First, they'd each find a stick or small tree branch. Then, they'd go to the bridge. On a count of three, they'd drop their sticks into the brook and watch them float under the bridge. Next, they would look over the other side of the bridge, waiting for the sticks to float out. The stick that floated out first was declared the winner.

Both princesses began to search the ground to find the best stick. While they searched, Sylvia followed them and happily sniffed the ground, almost as if she were searching, too. Her ears were pointed and alert.

Her eyes were sharp and bright. The girls knew that Sylvia was enjoying herself.

Olivia was looking for a certain kind of stick. It must not be too large, but not too small. It had to be straight, but not too skinny.

Juniper didn't know what kind of stick to pick. If she saw a stick and liked the way it looked, that was the stick she would choose.

"Look at this one!" said Juniper, taking up a stick from the forest floor.

"That stick is too crooked," said Olivia. "It will float crooked."

"What about this one?" asked Juniper, picking up a different stick.

"That one is too large," said Olivia. "It will float slowly."

When they had picked out their sticks, it was time to race. Olivia chose a smooth stick that was a little longer than her hand. Juniper chose a short and stubby stick. They dropped the sticks in the brook, then switched sides of the bridge to see which stick would win.

Olivia's stick floated out from under the bridge first and won the first race.

For the second race, Juniper decided to choose her stick more carefully. She wanted a stick like the one Olivia chose for the first race. And so Juniper found a very smooth stick, but it was also very long.

Olivia chose a new stick, too. It was a little shorter than her first one. The girls stood on the bridge and dropped their sticks. Then they switched sides to see the sticks float under the bridge.

Olivia's stick won again. She smiled smugly at Juniper.

Juniper wrinkled her brow. "I'll win the next one," she said.

This time, Juniper waited until Olivia had chosen her stick, and then she picked one that was just like it. They dropped their sticks into the brook. This time, the sticks both appeared from under the bridge at the same time.

"It's a tie!" said Juniper, happily.

"But I won the first two times," said Olivia. "So, I still win."

Juniper was about to argue with Olivia when she noticed that something was different.

"Hey," said Juniper, "Where's Sylvia?"

The last time Olivia had seen Sylvia she had been nosing around some shrubs by the brook. The last time Juniper had seen Sylvia, the little fox had been trotting farther into the forest. Both princesses had been so interested in their game, they didn't pay very much attention to their fox friend.

"Sylvia is probably hiding from us!" said Juniper.

"She's a sly one," said Olivia. "Let's find her!"

And so they looked all around. They checked behind the trees and under the shrubs. They searched along the path and around the bridge.

They didn't find Sylvia.

Next, Olivia and Juniper walked along the forest path and listened for Sylvia's happy yips and barks. They listened very carefully. They heard only the birds chirping, squirrels chattering, and leaves moving in the breeze.

"Maybe she ran back to Dad and Paul," said Olivia.

"Yeah," said Juniper. "Let's go and see."

The two princesses ran back down the path to find the grown-ups. This time, they ran faster than they had before.

The princesses were out of breath by the time they reached King Andrew and Paul. The two men were still strolling slowly, talking and laughing.

"Wow, I think we may have finally tired them out," said King Andrew, pointing to the princesses. "Look! They're so tired!"

"They've even outrun Sylvia," said Paul, with a laugh.

"Sylvia is not with you?" asked Olivia as she tried to catch her breath.

"No," said Paul. "Wasn't she with you?"

"She was with us for a while," said Olivia, "but now we can't find her."

Paul frowned a little.

"We'll find her," said King Andrew. "Where did you see her last?"

The princesses described stopping at the brook and playing the stick game on the bridge.

"To the bridge!" said King Andrew.

Together, they all started for the bridge.

"It hasn't been very long," said Paul as they walked. "Sylvia couldn't have gone far."

They called and shouted. "Sylvia! Sylvia, where are you?"

"Juniper and Olivia," said King Andrew, "will you keep searching along the path?"

"Yes, we will," said the Princesses.

"Good," said King Andrew. "Paul and I will search in the forest."

Olivia and Juniper ran on ahead. They stayed on the path, but they looked left and right. They called out for Sylvia.

But the two princesses saw no sign of Sylvia.

"She's not on the path," said Juniper. "She's probably over in the trees. We should go look over there." Juniper pointed to a shadowy area where there were lots of trees and brush.

"No, Juniper," said Olivia. She was a little bit older and more experienced. "We should stay on the path."

"Why?" asked Juniper.

"Because if we go off the path," Olivia answered, "we might get lost. Then Dad and Paul will have to find us, too."

Juniper frowned. She just wanted Sylvia to be found. She didn't like that Sylvia was missing. It gave her an unpleasant feeling of worry mixed with sadness. The day had been so fun, but it wasn't fun anymore.

Olivia didn't like it, either. Sylvia was their friend. Olivia was worried that Sylvia could be lost or hurt or afraid.

Still, the two princesses stayed on the trail and called for Sylvia. They scanned the forest, hoping to see their fox friend.

Meanwhile, King Andrew and Paul looked for Sylvia in the forest. But they didn't find her, either.

After a while, the sun began to set. Because of the trees, the forest seemed even darker at dusk than it usually did. The air got cooler, too.

When the sun was shining, the forest was pretty and fun. But as it grew dark, the forest changed. The trees seemed a little scary. The branches looked like long arms with thin fingers, just waiting to grab little princesses. The shadows were scary, too. What might be hiding there? It was also harder to find their way in the dark. They tripped and stumbled over stones and bumps in the trail.

"It's getting a little spooky in the forest," said Juniper.

"Yeah," said Olivia. "I hope we find Sylvia soon."

Both princesses were relieved when they met King Andrew and Paul again. They were both hoping that the king and Paul had found Sylvia. However, as they came nearer, the princesses saw the glum faces of the men. They knew that Sylvia had not been found.

"I'm afraid we're going to have to go home without Sylvia," said King Andrew sadly.

"We can't leave her out here alone!" protested Princess Olivia.

"We've looked all over and called for her," said Paul. "But there's been no sign of her."

"Has she ever run off like this before?" asked King Andrew.

"Yes, a few times," said Paul. "In fact, she did it a couple months ago. She was gone for an entire week. But she has always found her way home again."

"How can she find her way home when it's dark like this?" asked Juniper.

"Animals have much better senses than people," said Paul. "Foxes can see better than we can in the dark. They have good hearing and an amazing sense of smell. Sylvia can probably find her way home."

But the two sister princesses were still worried.

"I'm not leaving until we find Sylvia," said Juniper. Then, just in case it helped, she cupped her hands around her mouth and called, "Sylvia! Sylvia! Where are you?"

But there was no answer from Sylvia, and now it was growing even darker.

"Let's go home," said King Andrew. "Sylvia will probably find her way back home by morning."

Juniper didn't really want to go home without Sylvia, but she had to admit that she was starting to feel cold and hungry.

"Won't Sylvia be cold and hungry?" asked Olivia.

Juniper gasped, she hadn't even thought of that!

"Sylvia has a thick coat of fur that will keep her warm. Also, she knows how to find food," said Paul.

"She'll be okay," said King Andrew. "Don't forget, the forest was Sylvia's home before she was injured. This is where she lived before she lived with Paul.

"That's right," said Paul, agreeing with King Andrew.

However, both of the princesses noticed that Paul was no longer happy or laughing. They wondered if he was feeling as worried and sad as they were.

"Sylvia will be home by morning," Juniper declared.

"How do you know that?" asked King Andrew.

"Because that's what I want to happen!" said Juniper.

King Andrew took a breath. He thought he should explain to Juniper that things sometimes don't happen the way we want them to. Then he decided that it might not be a good idea to argue with Juniper while she was upset.

Who knows? thought King Andrew. *Maybe little Sylvia really will come home by morning.*

CHAPTER THREE
THE NEXT MORNING

THE PRINCESSES DID NOT SLEEP VERY WELL that night. Princess Juniper imagined Sylvia trying to find her way home in the cold and darkness. Princess Olivia kept thinking about how hungry Sylvia must be.

They both fell asleep after a while, but in the morning, they felt a little groggy and irritated.

"We need to check with Paul to see if Sylvia came home," said Olivia.

"Yes, right now!" said Juniper.

When they asked their mother, Queen Jennifer, if they could visit Paul in the village, she told them that there were several things they had to do first.

First, they had to have breakfast.

"Ugh, eating is such a pain," said Juniper.

"You usually love breakfast," said Olivia as she took a big bite of chocolate chip pancakes that Miss Beets, the castle chef, had made for them.

"I don't love it when it keeps me from finding our fox friend," said Juniper.

Second, they had to get dressed and ready for the day.

"Ugh, brushing my teeth is such a pain," said Juniper, except she had her toothbrush and toothpaste in her mouth, so it sounded more like, "Ugh, busheeg by feef us uch a fayne."

"The quicker we get ready," said Oliva, "the quicker we can go see Paul."

Third, Queen Jennifer said they must do their chores, too. They had to make their beds, tidy their rooms, and wash the breakfast dishes.

Juniper frowned. "Ugh, doing the dishes is—"

"Such a pain," said Olivia. "I know. But mom said we can go to Paul's candle store after this."

"Finally!" said Juniper.

"Hopefully, Sylvia came home last night," said Olivia. "And there will be nothing to worry about."

Princess Olivia hoped that was true. She wanted to get more sleep.

"Yes," said Juniper. "Sylvia will be there, or else."

"Or else what?" said Olivia.

"Or else I will be very angry!" said Juniper. She didn't like it when things didn't go her way. Princess Juniper didn't even want to think that Sylvia had not returned home.

At last the two princesses finished washing and drying the dishes. Then, just to make sure the job was done well, they used a dish towel to wipe up any water or soap bubbles that had spilled. They let their mom know that they were finally going to the candle shop, and then hurried there as fast as they could.

When they entered the candle shop in the village, Paul looked up at them from behind the store cabinet. There were dark circles under his eyes, and he looked tired. Princess Olivia suspected that he hadn't slept very well himself.

"Is Sylvia back?" asked Juniper.

Paul looked down and shook his head. "No, there is still no sign of her. If she's not back by this afternoon, I'm going to go look in the forest again."

"I'm sick of this," said Juniper. "I want her to come back right now!"

"You don't always get what you want, Juniper," said Olivia.

Juniper didn't understand this. She was feeling something she wasn't used to feeling.

"We hope you find Sylvia," said Princess Olivia. "Let us know if you do."

"Of course," said Paul.

The princesses walked back to Wildflower Castle a lot slower than they had walked to the candle shop.

"It's difficult to walk fast when you're feeling this sad," said Juniper.

Olivia nodded. "We had some good times with Sylvia. Maybe she's just made a new home in the forest."

"No," said Juniper firmly. "She's going to come back. I'll make her come back, you'll see."

"Juniper, we don't know where she is," said Olivia. "There's nothing we can do right now."

"Just you wait," said Juniper. "You'll see."

CHAPTER FOUR

THINKING LIKE A FOX

However, the truth was that Juniper didn't know what to do to help Sylvia the fox to get back home.

Princess Juniper herself had been lost on a few occasions. There was the time she'd been shopping with her mother at the shops in Wildflower Village. She saw a kitten run down an alley and she followed it. She didn't pay attention to where she was going. Juniper caught up to the kitten and held it for a while, but when she let it go, she didn't know where she was anymore. Worse, she didn't see her mother anywhere!

Being lost had given her a panicked feeling. She felt afraid and even started crying. But she remembered that the queen had taught her that if she ever got lost to look for another parent and ask for help.

Juniper had spotted a woman with two young kids. She worked up the courage to ask for help.

The lady just happened to know Queen Jennifer and had helped Juniper to look around the nearby streets to find her, and after just a few moments, they found her mother around the corner. Queen Jennifer had also been very worried, and she gave Juniper a big hug when they found her. Even before they had found her mother, Juniper had felt better knowing someone was helping her.

But Sylvia is a fox, thought Juniper. *She can't ask anyone for help because foxes don't talk.*

This was a real problem. How would Sylvia ever find her way home?

"It's time to think like a fox," said Juniper.

Juniper began pacing in her bedroom. "Think, think, think," she said, tapping her chin.

"I've got it!" she declared and ran to the kitchen.

Later that afternoon, Olivia decided to go outside to get some fresh air and to maybe collect some leaves and wildflowers to make a collage.

She was surprised to see Juniper outside. Juniper had a basket, a rubber ball, and one of Miss Beets' big mixing bowls.

"What are you doing?" asked Olivia, walking closer.

The mixing bowl was full of popcorn. In the basket there were chocolate candies and some cookies.

"I'm trying to get Sylvia to come back home," said Juniper.

Olivia scratched her head. "And how is this supposed to work?"

"Foxes have an excellent sense of smell," said Juniper. "She will come when she smells the snacks. Then I will show her the kickball, and she will want to play."

"I don't think this will work, Juniper." Olivia loved foxes and happened to know a great deal about them. "You don't know where Sylvia is. She's probably too far away to smell your snacks."

"She might be close," said Juniper.

"Maybe," replied Olivia, "but foxes don't eat these kinds of snacks. They don't like eating candy and cookies. They eat things they find in the forest."

"But I was thinking like a fox!" said Juniper. "I love candy and cookies and popcorn."

"You were thinking like a Juniper," said Olivia. "Sylvia's favorite things to eat are berries and mice."

"I could get some berries," said Juniper. "Do you think she would come if I had berries?"

"I already told you," said Olivia, "she's too far away." Then she shook her head and continued on to the castle playground.

Juniper scowled. Searching for Sylvia hadn't worked. Calling for her hadn't worked. And now trying to think like a fox wasn't going to work, either.

She put her hands on her hips and grumbled. She finally realized what she was feeling. She was angry!

Juniper was so angry that she kicked the mixing bowl. Popcorn went flying all over the grass. Then she tossed the basket full of snacks. The cookies and candy scattered everywhere. Juniper growled. She kicked the kickball. It sailed across the yard.

"Sylvia! You come home right now, and I mean it!" Juniper yelled as loudly as she could.

Her eyes scanned the path that led to the woods, but there still was no sign of Sylvia.

Juniper screamed! She stomped. She tore the ribbons from her hair and tossed them away.

She rolled around on the ground, growling, and shouting angrily. Juniper was covered in grass and stray leaves. Her hair was wild.

Then Juniper got up off the ground and took off one of her shoes! She was just about to throw it into the bushes, but just then someone walked up behind her and touched her on the shoulder.

CHAPTER FIVE
DEALING WITH FEELINGS

JUNIPER WAS STARTLED. She turned around to see who it was. It was her mother, Queen Jennifer.

Queen Jennifer looked at Juniper's face. The princess's face was red as a tomato!

Queen Jennifer looked at the grass. It was covered with popcorn and candy and cookies!

Queen Jennifer noticed Juniper's hair. The ribbons were gone and her hair was very messy!

Queen Jennifer saw that Juniper was ready to throw her shoe into the bushes!

Queen Jennifer said, "Something tells me that you are quite angry. What's wrong, Juniper?"

"I am angry!" shouted Juniper and she kicked the bowl of snacks again. "I'm mad! I'm furious!"

"Juniper," said Queen Jennifer, "Miss Beets would not be happy if she saw you kicking her serving bowl or tossing her homemade cookies around."

"I'm angry!" Juniper repeated.

"I can tell!" said Queen Jennifer. "But can you tell me why?"

"Because—because—" started Juniper. However, she actually wasn't quite sure why she was so angry. But that didn't make any sense, because she was feeling a very strong emotion!

"Because Sylvia won't come home!" Juniper finally said. "We've tried and tried to get her home, and she just won't come back, and that makes me—angry! Really angry! And Olivia won't help. And Paul and father won't help. No one else is even trying to get Sylvia back home."

Queen Jennifer nodded and put her arm around Juniper. "Put your shoe back on and come with me. Let's take a little walk."

They walked down the stone walkway that led to the castle courtyard. Juniper felt like she was burning inside, like there was a bunch of steam inside her that wanted to come out through her nose and ears.

"Sometimes," said Queen Jennifer. "When we are angry, it's really because we are feeling other feelings."

"I don't understand," said Juniper.

"Sometimes, certain feelings make us uncomfortable," said Queen Jennifer. "Sometimes, we have strong feelings and don't know what to do about them."

Juniper looked at Queen Jennifer and listened.

"Tell me, Juniper," said Queen Jennifer, "are you worried about Sylvia?"

"Yes," said Juniper, this time without shouting. "I

am worried about her because I don't know where she is."

"I understand," said Queen Jennifer. "But what can you do about that?"

"It seems like there's nothing I can do!" said Juniper. "We have searched, and we have called out, and I even offered Sylvia some snacks. But she still will not come home!"

"It's normal to feel sad and worried about your fox friend," said Queen Jennifer. "Do you also feel a little afraid?"

Juniper thought about this and realized that she did feel afraid. She was afraid that she might never see Sylvia again, and she was also afraid that Sylvia might be hurt or lonely or hungry. Juniper was even a little afraid that maybe someday she herself would be missing again, like she had been that one time in the village. What if she was lost and no one was able to find her?

"Yes," admitted Juniper. "I feel sad and worried and afraid."

"It's okay to feel that way," said Queen Jennifer. "And because you don't know what to do, you're feeling angry, too."

Juniper blinked her eyes and thought about this.

But then Juniper's eyes filled up with tears, and she was sure that if she tried to explain what she was thinking about that she would start to cry. Juniper didn't like to cry. It made her face hot and her nose run. So instead of explaining what she was afraid of and how it made her sad, Juniper just nodded her head.

"Well," said Queen Jennifer. "I think it's perfectly reasonable that you might feel sad and afraid and scared and even angry because Sylvia is missing. I feel those same things."

"You do?" asked Juniper. The queen was always so calm, it was hard to imagine her ever being afraid.

"I do," said Queen Jennifer. "And you know what? It's good that we feel this way. Feelings are good. Your feelings mean that Sylvia is very special to you. She is a good friend. You wouldn't be feeling these things so strongly, if you didn't have such a great friendship with Sylvia."

"You're not angry at me for being angry?" asked Juniper.

"It's normal to feel angry sometimes," said Queen Jennifer. "Everyone feels angry. But we still have to be responsible for our actions. So if we've said something unkind or done something we shouldn't have, we need to fix it."

"So, I need to clean up the mess I made," said Princess Juniper.

Queen Jennifer smiled. "I think that would be a good idea. I'll help you."

They walked back, and as they did so, Princess Juniper realized she didn't feel so angry anymore. She was still a little sad and worried, but taking a little walk and talking with her mom had helped.

They found the mess Juniper had made. Luckily, the bowl wasn't damaged. They were just finishing picking up the last of the spilled food when they heard Paul shouting and running down the path to them. He was waving his arm and trying to get their attention.

Princess Juniper thought maybe he'd found Sylvia, but her heart sank a little when she realized there was no fox with him.

CHAPTER SIX
THE DISCOVERY

Olivia must have heard Paul as well, because she came running from the playground. Together, Juniper, Olivia, and Queen Jennifer ran to meet Paul. He was out of breath. He leaned over and rested his hands on his knees. Then he held up a finger to let everyone know that he needed a moment to catch his breath.

After a while, Paul stood up and said, "I ran all the way here to tell you—!"

"Tell us what? Tell us what?" cried the princesses.

But Paul was still out of breath. "I went back to the woods," he said, panting. "To search for Sylvia."

"Yes? Yes? And then what?" cried the princesses.

"Let Paul catch his breath, girls," said Queen Jennifer.

Paul was still breathing hard. "I just had to let you know—!"

"What? What?" said the princesses. They were jumping up and down on their tippie-toes.

"I found Sylvia!" said Paul at last.

The princesses cheered and jumped even higher.

"Where is she? Where is she?" cried the girls.

"Yes, Paul," said Queen Jennifer. "Where is Sylvia?"

Paul shook his head. "You'll never believe it! I can't explain it! You have to come with me to see! Go and get King Andrew and then come with me to the forest!"

"You wait here!" said Queen Jennifer. "I will go find King Andrew, and we will return with unicorns to ride!"

Paul agreed, and the queen and princesses dashed away. After a few minutes, they returned with King Andrew and the unicorns. They all climbed onto their unicorns, and in an instant, they were galloping down the path and into the forest.

"This is wonderful," said King Andrew as he rode along with Juniper. "I've been so worried about Sylvia."

Princess Juniper was surprised to hear this. The king had been worried, too?

Paul rode ahead down the path. The others followed him on their unicorns. They all wanted to know what Paul had found, but he wouldn't say.

"You have to see this to believe it!" said Paul, laughing and smiling. "You must see it for yourselves!"

In fact, Paul laughed and smiled so much that everyone else began to smile and laugh.

"Oh, I simply can't wait to see!" said Queen Jennifer.

"What could it be?" cried Olivia.

"I want to know!" shouted Juniper.

King Andrew laughed. "This is very exciting!" he said.

Soon they came to a peaceful place in the forest. It was shady and quiet. They could hear the brook nearby, flowing through the forest.

Paul stopped his unicorn on the path. The others rode up and stopped.

"Juniper? Olivia?" said Paul. "Do you know what a burrow is?"

"I do," said Olivia, who was very smart and had read a great deal. "A burrow is a hole in the ground dug by animals."

"Yes, that's right!" said Paul. "And do you know what animals dig burrows?"

"Rabbits, I think," said Juniper. "And squirrels."

"And foxes!" said Olivia excitedly. She really did know a lot about foxes.

"Yes!" said Paul. "Sylvia's made herself a burrow out here in the forest."

"Why would she do that?" Princess Juniper asked.

Olivia gasped. "I think I know why!" She couldn't wait to see if she was right.

Paul got down from his unicorn. The others did, too. Then they told the unicorns to graze on some forest grasses.

"Stay here," said Queen Jennifer to the unicorns. "We will be back shortly."

They followed Paul into the forest. After they

walked for a few minutes, Paul stopped and turned to the princesses.

"Now we must keep our voices soft," he said.

"Why?" asked Juniper.

"Just trust me," said Paul. "I know you will be happy to see Sylvia again, but you mustn't shout or yell. Not right now."

"Okay," said Juniper.

Paul pointed to something up ahead in the forest. "Now," he said, "look there!"

The princesses looked where Paul pointed. At first, they just saw trees and shrubs, but then they saw it. Sylvia's burrow! Sylvia must have seen them. Or maybe she had smelled or heard them. Sylvia stepped out of the burrow and happily pranced over to them. She jumped up on the princesses and licked their faces.

Olivia and Juniper grinned and giggled. They were so happy to see their fox friend and to know that she was safe! And yet they did as Paul said. They did not raise their voices.

"But why did she make a burrow out here?" Princess Juniper asked in a quiet voice.

"Ask Sylvia," whispered Paul, "and she will show you!"

"Sylvia," said Juniper, "why did you make a burrow? We were so worried."

Sylvia licked Juniper's hand and took a few steps toward the burrow. Then she looked over her shoulder at the princesses and tossed her head. She was telling them to come closer. Juniper and Olivia stepped forward.

Inside the burrow, there were four tiny foxes!

"Sylvia has babies!" said Juniper. She might have raised her voice a little that time.

"Sylvia has *kits!*" said Olivia, her voice quiet. "Baby foxes are called kits!"

"May we hold them?" asked Juniper. "May we pet them?"

Sylvia answered with a "yip yip!"

"I think she means yes," said Paul with a big smile.

"Be very careful, girls," said Queen Jennifer.

The girls sat down outside the burrow and gently held Sylvia's kits. They patted them gently.

"They're so cute! They're so beautiful!" said the girls.

Paul's smile grew even bigger.

"Will you bring Sylvia and her kits back to the village?" Juniper asked.

"No," said Paul. "I think Sylvia will stay in the forest. We are still her friends, and we can visit sometimes. I was worried and upset when I didn't know where she was, but she is safe and happy here. And that makes me happy, too."

"It makes me happy, also," said King Andrew.

"And me," said Queen Jennifer.

"And me," said Olivia.

Juniper thought about it. She had gotten very upset when Sylvia was missing. Juniper wanted Sylvia to come home, no matter what. Juniper felt worried, afraid, uncomfortable, and even angry. But now Juniper knew that some things happened no matter how she felt about them. That was okay. Now she knew a little bit more about what to do with big, upsetting feelings.

And so Juniper nodded and said, "And me, too!"

COULD YOU DO ME A FAVOR?

Thank you for reading The Princess and the Fox. I hope you enjoyed it!

Could you do me a small favor? Would you leave a review of this book with the retailer where it was purchased? Reviews help me to reach new readers. I would really appreciate it!

—A.M. Luzzader

WWW.AMLUZZADER.COM

- blog
- freebies
- newsletter
- contact info

ABOUT THE AUTHOR

A.M. Luzzader is an award-winning children's book author who writes chapter books and middle grade books. She specializes in writing books for preteens including *A Mermaid in Middle Grade and Arthur Blackwood's Scary Stories for Kids who Like Scary Stories*

A.M. decided she wanted to write fun stories for

kids when she was still a kid herself. By the time she was in fourth grade, she was already writing short stories. In fifth grade, she bought a typewriter at a garage sale to put her words into print, and in sixth grade she added illustrations.

Now that she has decided what she wants to be when she grows up, A.M. writes books for kids full time. She was selected as the Writer of the Year in 2019-2020 by the League of Utah Writers.

A.M. is the mother of a 12-year-old and a 15-year-old who often inspire her stories. She lives with her husband and children in northern Utah. She is a devout cat person and avid reader.

A.M. Luzzader's books are appropriate for ages 5-12. Her chapter books are intended for kindergarten to third grade, and her middle grade books are for third grade through sixth grade. Find out more about A.M., sign up to receive her newsletter, and get special offers at her website: www.amluzzader.com.

facebook.com/a.m.luzzader

instagram.com/amluzzader

ABOUT THE ILLUSTRATOR

Anna M. Clark is an artist who loves to draw, tell stories, and buy journals. She has worked as a baker, a math tutor, a security guard, an art teacher, and works now as an illustrator and artist!

She has traveled through Southeast Asia, was born on Halloween (the best holiday ever), and loves to create large chalk art murals. Anna lives with her husband in their cute apartment in Logan, Utah, with their beautiful basil plant.

Explore more of Anna M. Clark's work and her current projects at her website: annamclarkart.com.

OTHER BOOKS BY
A.M. Luzzader

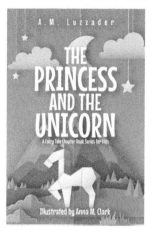
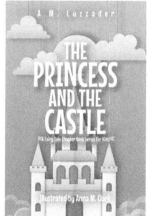

A Fairy Tale Chapter Book Series for Kids

For ages 6-10

OTHER BOOKS BY
A.M. Luzzader

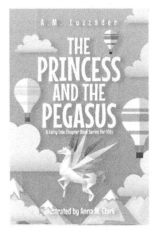
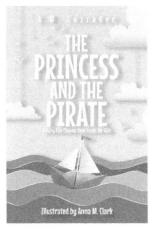

A Fairy Tale Chapter Book Series for Kids

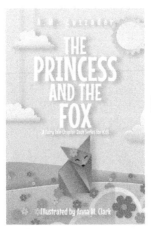

For ages
6-10

OTHER BOOKS BY
A.M. Luzzader

Pet Magic

For ages
6-10

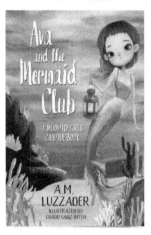
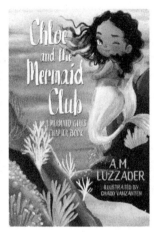

OTHER BOOKS BY
A.M. Luzzader

A Magic School for Girls Chapter Book

For ages
6-8

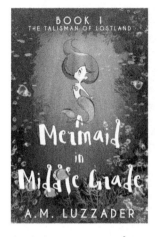
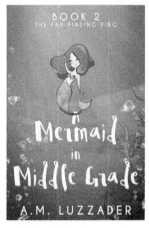

Made in the USA
Las Vegas, NV
03 May 2023

71476143R00049